A Pilgrimage to Beethoven

Richard Wagner

Contents

A PILGRIMAGE TO BEETHOVEN

BY

Richard Wagner

A PILGRIMAGE TO BEETHOVEN
PUBLISHERS' PREFACE.

RICHARD WAGNER, the famous musical composer, experienced perhaps the hardest time of his life in Paris. He left Riga, where he had been engaged as leader at a theatre in the year 1839, and taking passage on board a sailing vessel reached Boulogne-sur-mer after an adventurous sea-voyage, which suggested to him the idea of composing "The Flying Dutchman."

In Boulogne-sur-mer Wagner met Meyerbeer, who promised to do all he could for him in Paris.

Without any other recommendation than that of Meyerbeer, Wagner entered Paris, with little money but great expectations. On the strength of Meyerbeer's recommendation the director of the Theatre de la Renaissance promised to put on the stage one of Wagner's compositions, which was being translated by M. Dumersan. But before the translation was completed the Theatre de la Renaissance was bankrupt, and Richard Wagner was that much poorer in his hopes.

There were a number of famous musicians in Paris—Habeneck, Halévy, and others—but none of them attracted Wagner, who had no sympathy for artists whose sole object was to be counted among the lions of musical composition, and then to write operas for the purpose of making as much money as possible. He thought most of Berlioz, in spite of his repulsive character, because he at least did not compose for the sake of money; but Wagner never sought the friendship of Berlioz, of whom he said that "he lacked the genuine sense of art."

Finding no sympathetic friends among musicians, Wagner frequented the circles of authors, painters, and scholars. And his disgust with the lack of idealism in the musical world of Paris, together with his straitened circumstances, which sometimes bordered on actual destitution, made his sojourn in Paris very gloomy; but his sorry experience only served to purify his love for music, and the mere sight of the public which took delight in the frivolous melodies of the Italian operas made him think more seriously about the high purpose of genuine music. He became more and more conscious of his ideals, and when requested by M. Schlesinger to write for the Gazette Musicale he wrote several articles, among which the most beautiful is his novelette, A Pilgrimage to Beethoven.

The success of this first literary attempt of Wagner induced him to write several other articles on German music, including "The Virtuosi and the Artists," "The Artist and the Public," being a talk on music in the form of a dialogue, "A Happy Evening," and "Rossini's Stabat Mater." Another sketch, entitled An End in Paris, which was intended to be a continuation of his novelette, A Pilgrimage to Beethoven, is written in a profoundly melancholy mood, and seems to convey the lesson of Schopenhauer's pessimism that a genius is not fit to live in this miserable world, but must die of starvation.

In the first volume of his collected works Wagner published all the literary essays on music written at that time, as the Posthumous Papers of the hero of his first novelette. In none of the essays, however, did Wagner reach the same height of poetic inspiration as in his Pilgrimage to Beethoven. Most of them are fair articles on musical subjects; the one which discusses Rossini's Stabat Mater is a vigorous and well-written, although decidedly unjust, accusation of a rival. They all may claim to be above mediocrity and all are worth reading; but the main interest we can take in them consists in the fact that they were written by a great composer.

The sketch, "A Happy Evening," contains several beautiful passages on music which are worth quoting. Wagner criticises those musical critics who confound the languages of music and of poetry, trying, for instance, to interpret Beethoven's "Symphony in A sharp" as a peasant marriage. "Music," Wagner says, "expresses that which is eternal, infinite, and ideal. Music does not "express the passion, the love, the yearning of this or that individual, in this or that situation. It expresses passion, love, and "yearning themselves, and, indeed, in an infinitely manifold variety of motives, whose exclusive peculiarity is conditioned in the "nature of music, and is foreign and inexpressible in any other "kind of speech." (Ges. Werke, Vol. I. p. 183.)

The form in which this essay, "A Happy Evening,"

is dressed, is that of a dialogue between two enthusiastic musicians, in which one of them says: "Blessed be the God who created the spring and music." (Ibid., p. 173.) Wagner makes one of them sum up the gist of their conversation in these words, which are the conclusion of that "happy evening": "Long live good fortune; "long live joy; long live the courage that animates us in the struggle with our fate; long live the victory which a nobler consciousness gains over the infamy of all that is vulgar; long live that "love which requites our courage ; long live friendship which supports our faith; long live hope, the ally of our presages; long "live the day ; long live the night; a greeting to the sun ; a greeting to the stars; thrice greeted be Music and her high-priests! "Eternally adored and worshipped be God, the God of joy and "of happiness, the God who created music. Amen!"

With all such passages, which are beautiful in themselves, these various essays can only be forced into a unity with Wagner's novelette, A Pilgrimage to Beethoven, and this is true most of all of the continuation of the novelette, An End in Paris. This latter is even jarring.

While the little tale, A Pilgrimage to Beethoven, reaches the highest pitch of noble enthusiasm for music, in which all the misery of this world appears transfigured, its continuation,

An End in Paris, is so full of discord that all beauty of the idealism of art is drowned in the sufferings that precede the terrible act of suicide. The two sketches have been written in two different moods, and they do not belong together. We can understand how Richard Wagner, oppressed with cares and sorrows, came to write the tragic tale, An End in Paris, but we cannot approve of spoiling the first novel, A Pilgrimage to Beethoven, by attaching to it the ghastly story of an unsuccessful genius, who, by overestimating his own talents, lives in a fool's paradise and becomes at last, when starvation stares him in the face, a prey to despair.

A most beautiful passage, in this otherwise terrible story, is unquestionably the dying musician's confession of faith which he expresses in his last will as follows:

'I believe in God, Mozart, and Beethoven, and also in their "disciples and apostles. I believe in the Holy Ghost and in the "truth of the invisible Art. I believe that Art proceeds from God "and lives in the hearts of all enlightened men. I believe that whoever has once revelled in the lofty enjoyments of this high Art "will be her devotee forever and can never deny her I believe "that all can become blessed through Art, and that, therefore, "everybody should be permitted to die of starvation for her sake. "I believe that I shall be highly beatified through death. I believe "that I was a discord on earth which through death shall be gloriously resolved in purity. I believe in a last judgment which will "condemn terribly all those who have dared to practise usury in this "world with that high and chaste Art, those who prostituted and "dishonored her through the depravity of their hearts and vile "greed for sensuality! I believe that all such evil doers will be "condemned to listen to their own music for all eternity. Yet I "believe that the faithful disciples of this high Art will be "transfigured, clad in heavenly garments of sunny and scented "melodies, and will be united with the divine source of all harmony "forever and aye. May a merciful lot fall to me! Amen."

Having extracted from Wagner's essays those passages which we deem beautiful and most expressive, we abstain from translating and publishing the story, An End in Paris, because we are convinced that the beauty of the novelette, A Pilgrimage to Beethoven, can only be spoiled by receiving a false and inappropriate setting. In letting the novelette stand by itself, as it was first conceived by Richard Wagner, we believe that we restore it to its original beauty. It is a most exquisite gem of the poetic imagination of a great composer, and deserves to be widely read and known all over the world. May this translation make it popular all over the English-speaking world and help the spread of a love of true Art and genuine Music.

PAUL CARUS, Manager of the Open Court Publishing Co.

A PILGRIMAGE TO BEETHOVEN.

OINDIGENCE! thou care-bringer! protectress divine of the German musician (unless he have reached the haven of director at some court-theatre)! O, carking Indigence! as I ever do, so let me now in this reminiscence from my life first bring dutiful obeisance to thy praise and honor! Let me sing of thee, thou steadfast companion of my life! Always loyal, never hast thou forsaken me! With a strong palm, thou hast warded from me all sudden shocks of propitious luck; and ever against the onerous glances of sunny Fortuna hast thou protected me! With an impenetrable veil hast thou always benignantly hidden from my sight the vain riches of this world! Receive thou all my gratitude for thine indefatigable constancy. But if it may be, pray do thou at length find some other foster-child than me. For indeed I should— if it were only for the sake of curiosity—like to learn from personal experience, what manner of existence I might manage to lead without thee. At the least—so I beseech thee—go thou and plague with most especial cunning our political dreamers, those madmen, who are determined in spite of everything to unite our dear Germany under a single sceptre : For then there would be but one single court-theatre, and hence a place for but one single Kapellmeister! What then would become of all my hopes, my dear ambitions, which even now are dim before my eyes, and, I dread, are slowly fading— even now, when I can count so many German court-theatres. But ah! I see that I grow impious. Forgive, O thou divine protectress, the blasphemous wish which just escaped me. 'Twas but momentary; for thou seest within my heart, and well thou knowest how wholly thine I am, and ever shall be, though it came to pass that there were a thousand court-theatres in Germany! Amen!

I never undertake a thing, without first offering up this daily prayer, and so I breathe it here before I begin the story of my pilgrimage to Beethoven.

But to provide for the possibility that this important

autobiographical record may find publication after my demise, I consider it necessary to tell who I am. Else much therein might appear obscure. Let my executors and the world, therefore, know these things:

My native place is a city of fair size in Central Germany. I am not quite certain what the plans of my people for my future had been. All that I recall is, that one evening I heard one of Beethoven's symphonies for the first time; that I was taken with fever in consequence, was ill for some time, and, when I had recovered, had become a musician.

I suppose it is because of this circumstance that although I have since then learned to know and appreciate much other music that is beautiful, I have, foremost, loved, and honored, and adored Beethoven. I knew no greater delight than that of yielding myself wholly up to him,—of allowing myself to sink, as it were, away into the depths of his genius, until I should finally imagine that I was a part thereof; and even as such a tiny part I would begin to esteem myself, have more elevated conceptions and opinions, and, in a word, to be what the wiseacres usually call a simpleton. This delusion was of a very gentle sort, and it did no harm to any one. The daily bread which I ate during this period of my life was very dry, my wine very thin and watery; for the giving of music-lessons does not earn much of an income where I live, my dear executors and public!

I had been living thus in my little garret for some time when suddenly, one day, it occurred to me that the man whose creations I adored above everything else, was still living. I could not understand how it was that I had not thought of this before. It had never suggested itself to me as possible that Beethoven could actually stand before one, that he could eat and breathe like an ordinary mortal. And here he was, living in Vienna; and he, too, was a poor German musician like myself!

From that instant my peace of mind was gone. All my thoughts turned into the one wish, to see Beethoven! Never Mussulman more devoutly yearned to make the pilgrimage to the grave of his prophet, than I to the humble chamber where Beethoven dwelt.

But how should I manage to carry out such a design? The journey to Vienna was a long one, and money was required to make it; whilst I, poor wretch, was hardly earning enough to keep body and soul together. It was painfully evident that I should have to devise some extraordinary measures, if I hoped to get the necessary travelling-money together. I had composed several sonatas for the piano, in the master's style; these I carried to a publisher. But the man curtly gave me to understand that I was a simpleton with my sonatas. He advised me, that, if I expected in time to earn a few dollars with compositions of this kind, I should first undertake to make something of a reputation with galops and potpourris. I shuddered at the thought. But my longing to see Beethoven conquered. I composed galops and potpourris. But during all this time, from very shame, I could not bring myself to even so much as look at my Beethoven; I shrank in horror from the desecration.

Unfortunately, however, I failed at first to get any compensation at all for these sacrifices of innocence. For although he published them, my publisher said he could not pay me for them until I had secured somewhat of a name. Again I shuddered, I succumbed to despair. But despair yielded some excellent galops. I really got some money for them; and at length the time came when I believed I had amassed enough to execute my plans. But in the meantime two years had passed away; and during all that time I was in mortal dread lest Beethoven might die before I had achieved a name with my galops and potpourris. Thank heavens! he survived the grandeur of my fame. Sainted Beethoven! forgive me for this fame; for I sought and won it that I might see you.

Ah, what genuine ecstasy! I had attained my goal! Who in the wide world happier than I! Now, at last, I could throw my bundle over my shoulder and start on my pilgrimage to Beethoven. I felt a holy thrill as I marched through the city-gates and directed my course to the South. Only too gladly would I have taken a seat in one of the stage-coaches. Not because I dreaded the toil of foot-travel (for what tribulations would I not eagerly have borne for this dear object!), but because then I should the sooner have gotten to Beethoven. Alas! I had as yet accomplished too little for my celebrity as a galop-composer to be able to pay the costly fare. Accordingly, I resolutely faced every hardship, deeming myself lucky since they terminated in bringing me to Beethoven. O, how I raved! and dreamed! Never lover knew greater bliss, returning after a long separation to the love of his youth.

After a time I entered the beautiful land of Bohemia, the home of the harp-players and wandering singers. In one little town I ran across a company of these nomad musicians. They formed a little orchestra, made up of a bass, two violins, two horns, a clarinet, and a flute. There were three women with them; one was a harp-player; the other two were singers and had fine voices. They played dances and sang folk-songs; people gave them money, and they journeyed on. Later I chanced upon them again in a pretty and shady nook, just off the highway. They were bivouacking and having their dinner. I joined them, telling them that I, too, was a musician. We were soon on good terms. Since they played dances, I asked them, rather timidly, if they had ever yet played any of my galops. The splendid fellows! they had never heard of my galops! What a world of relief this knowledge afforded me!

Then I asked if they did not play some other music besides dance-music.

"To be sure we do!" they answered, "but for ourselves

only, not for the people who consider themselves above us."

They got out their music. I remarked among it the grand septette of Beethoven; surprised I asked them if they played that, too.

"And why not, pray?" the oldest of them rejoined. "Joseph's hand is disabled so that he cannot play the second violin; or we should take great pleasure in playing it for you right now."

Enraptured, I seized Joseph's violin and promised to the best of my ability to supply his place; and we began the septette.

What a delightful experience! Here, upon a Bohemian highway, beneath the open heaven, to hear Beethoven's septette played by common strolling musicians, with a purity, a precision, and a depth of sentiment, as seldom by masterful virtuosi! Great Beethoven! we brought thee a worthy offering!

We were right in the midst of the finale, when—the road here taking a winding course up the hill—an elegant travelling coach noiselessly approached and drew up close by us. A remarkably tall and remarkably blond young man lay extended at full length within the wagon, harkened with considerable attentiveness to our music, and then, drawing a note-book from his pocket, jotted down something therein. Then, after suffering a gold piece to drop from the wagon, he gave orders to his people to drive on, addressing them briefly in English, from which I knew that he must be an Englishman.

The interruption spoiled our musical mood, though it occurred fortunately after we had finished the septette. With emotion I embraced my friends and wished to accompany them. But they told me their course turned off from the main road at this point and took them across fields to their native village to which they were returning on one of their periodical visits. Had it not been that Beethoven himself was waiting for me, I certainly should have gone thither with them, too. As it was, we parted, uttering our farewells with mutual feeling. I remembered, later on, that no one had picked up the Englishman's gold-piece.

At the next inn,—where I turned in to rest my weary limbs,—I found the Englishman, seated at a good meal. He examined me attentively for a time, and at length addressed me in passable German:

"Where are your companions?"

"Gone home," I said.

"Get out your violin and play something more," he continued. "Here's money."

I was offended. I said curtly that I did not play for money, had furthermore no violin, and explained to him briefly how it was that I had happened to be in the company of the musicians.

"They were good players," observed the Englishman. "And the symphony of Beethoven was very good, too."

I was struck with this remark. I asked him if he did anything in the way of music himself.

"Yes," he replied. "I play the flute twice a week. Thursdays I blow the bugle. And Sundays I compose."

That was certainly a great deal, and I marvelled. I had never in all my life heard of strolling English musicians. I reasoned, therefore, that they must be in very easy circumstances, if they did their strolling in such handsome equipages.—I asked him if he was a musician by profession.

For some time I got no reply. Finally, drawling slowly, he exerted himself to say that he had much money.

I saw my error, for evidently the question had offended him. Mortified, I became silent, and went on eating my modest meal.

The Englishman, after another long scrutiny of my person, began again:

"Do you know Beethoven?" he asked.

I replied that I had never as yet been at Vienna, that I was just then on my way thither, and that my object in going there was to satisfy the dearest wish I had, that of seeing the adored master.

"Where are you from?" he asked.

"From L. ..."

"That's but a short distance off. I come from England, and my object, too, is to make the acquaintance of Beethoven. We will both make his acquaintance. He is a very celebrated composer."

"What a wonderful coincidence," I thought to myself. What very different kinds of folk dost thou not attract, sublime master! On foot and in wagon they flock to thee. My Englishman began to interest me; but I own that I little envied him his fine equipage. My toilsome pilgrimage, so it appeared to me, was the more holy and devout of the two; and I felt that when we reached our goal, mine must surely bring more joy to me than his to him, who made his progress thither in pomp and pride.

Just then the postilion blew his horn. The Englishmen rode away, after calling to me that he should see Beethoven before me.

I had been trudging after him but a few hours when I unexpectedly came upon him again. It was along the road. One of his wagon-wheels had broken down. He was still seated within the wagon, imperturbably tranquil, his servant up behind, unheeding that the wagon had pitched heavily on its side. I learned that they were waiting for the postilion, who had hastened to a village lying some distance away, to fetch a smith. They had been waiting a long while. And, as the servant spoke English only, I resolved to go myself to the village and fetch both postilion and smith. Just as I expected, I found the postilion in the tavern, where he sat at liquor, with little care for the Englishman. But I soon brought him and the smith back to the wagon. The injury was repaired. The Englishman promised to remember me to Beethoven and—rode away.

How very much surprised I was, on the next day, to overtake him on the highway again. His wheel was all right this time ; he had calmly stopped in the middle of the road and was reading in a book. He seemed to feel some satisfaction as he saw me come plodding along on my journey.

"I have been waiting here a great many hours," he said. "For right here it occurred to me that I had done wrong in not inviting you to ride with me to Beethoven. Riding is much better than walking. Come, get into the wagon."

Again I was surprised. And really, for a moment, I was undecided whether to accept his offer or not. But quickly I recalled the vow which I had made the day before, as I saw the Englishman speed away in his carriage. I had vowed absolutely to make my pilgrimage afoot. I now declared it aloud. With that, it was the Englishman's turn to be surprised; he could make nothing of me. He repeated his offer, adding again that he had been waiting a good many hours for me, although his journey had already been very greatly delayed by the work of having his broken wheel more thoroughly repaired in the place where he had lain the night before. I remained firm, however, and he rode, wondering, away.

To tell the truth, I had secretly begun to feel an aversion for him. For, like a gloomy premonition, the thought forced itself on me that this Englishman would yet cause me a great deal of trouble. And besides, both his admiration of Beethoven and his intention to form the acquaintance of the maestro looked more like a rich exquisite's hobby, than the deep and keen thirst of an enthusiastic soul. Accordingly, I chose to avoid him, that my devout yearning might not be unhallowed by any communion with him.

But, as if my destiny were determined to admonish me in advance of the fateful companionship I would yet come to with this gentleman, I met him still again in the evening of the same day, stopping in front of a hotel,— waiting for me, so it seemed. For he sat in the forward seat, looking down the road in my direction, whence he had himself come.

"Sir," he said, "I have again been waiting many hours for you. Will you ride with me to Beethoven? "

This time a secret horror began to mingle with my surprise. It was impossible otherwise to explain this strange insistence to serve me, than that the Englishman, observing my increasing aversion for him, was determined to force himself upon me, for the purpose of compassing my ruin. With unfeigned impatience, I again refused his offer. Contemptuously,he exclaimed :

"Confound it! I don't believe you think so very much of Beethoven. I shall soon see him." And away he flew at a rapid pace.

As it turned out, I did not see this insular citizen again during the still very considerable part remaining of the road to Vienna. I entered the streets of that city at last. My pilgrimage was ended. With what feelings I entered this Mecca of my creed! All the fatigues of my long and toilsome journey were forgotten. I was in my haven, within the walls which enclosed Beethoven.

My emotion was too deep for me to think of prosecuting my purpose at once. I did, it is true, immediately inquire after the residence of Beethoven, but it was merely that I might get lodgings in the neighborhood. Almost exactly opposite the house there was a hotel, not too pretentious. I took a small chamber in the fifth story, and there I prepared myself for the greatest event of my life, a call on Beethoven.

When I had rested two days, and fasted and prayed, without, however, bestowing so much as a single glance of sight-seeing on Vienna, I summoned courage, went forth from the hotel and across the street to the famous house. I was told that Beethoven was not at home. Secretly, I was glad to hear it, for it afforded me time to collect myself again. But when I had received the same reply four more times in the course of the day, each time in a certain increasing asperity of tone, I made up my mind that this was an unlucky day, and morosely abandoned my call for that day.

As I was returning to the hotel, lo! my Englishman, up on the first floor, nodded pleasantly down to me.

"Have you seen Beethoven?" he called out.

"Not yet; he wasn't in," I replied, surprised at meeting him again.

He came out to meet me in the stairway and pressed

me, with a marked degree of friendliness, to enter his apartment.

"I saw you go five times to-day to Beethoven's house. I have now been here many days, and have taken quarters in this odious hotel, simply to be near Beethoven. Believe me, it is very difficult to get a word with Beethoven; the gentleman seems to have whims and plenty of them. I made six efforts the first trial, and was each time denied. Now I rise very early in the morning and sit till late in the evening, watching at my window to see when Beethoven goes abroad. But the gentleman appears never to go abroad."

"And so you believe that Beethoven has been home all day to-day, too, and that he purposely had me refused?"

"Certainly. You and I, both of us have been refused. I am very sore over it. For I have come hither, not to see Vienna, but Beethoven."

This was very disconsolate information for me. Nevertheless, I tried my fortune again on the following day; once more without effect,—the gates of heaven remained closed against me.

My Englishman, who continued to watch my efforts from his window, always with the closest attention, had now gotten the assurance, from inquiries he had made, that Beethoven did not live on the side toward the street. He was very much irritated, but his persistence never flagged.

For my part, my patience was soon exhausted. For I had far more urgent reasons to feel thus. A week had gradually passed by and still I had not accomplished my design; and the little fortune from my galops would not permit of a very long stay in Vienna. Little by little I began to lose hope.

I confided my sorrows to mine host. He smiled and promised to let me know the cause of my ill success, if I would vow not to tell it to the Englishman. Half suspecting now what had been my evil star, I gave him the promise he demanded.

"Well, you see," mine honest host then said, "there is a continual stream of Englishmen hither, who wish to see Beethoven and try to get an introduction to him. He is so irritated by it, and he feels such wrath against the insistence of these people, that he has made it impossible for a stranger to get to him. He is different from other men and we must pardon him for this course. It is a very good thing for my hotel, however; for the house is usually filled with Englishmen, who, because of the difficulty of gaining admittance to Beethoven, are compelled to be my guests for a much longer time than otherwise would be the case. But since you have promised not to frighten these good people away, I hope to find a way whereby you may reach Herr Beethoven."

This was edifying. I could not attain my object, then, because, poor soul, I was taken for an Englishman! O, my premonition was right; that Englishman was my ruin!

I was for leaving the hotel upon the instant. For, no doubt, every one who stopped in it was taken for an Englishman, over in Beethoven's house; and that alone sufficed to put me under the ban. Still, the promise of the inn-keeper, that he would provide me with an opportunity to see and speak to Beethoven, restrained me.

In the meantime, the Englishman—whom I now detested from the very bottom of my heart—had been trying the efficacy of all kinds of intrigue and bribery;

always, however, without result.

Thus several more days passed fruitlessly away, during which the profits of my galops melted visibly; when mine host whispered in confidence to me that I could not fail of seeing Beethoven if I betook myself to a certain beer-garden which he was accustomed to frequent at a particular hour. At the same time I received from my adviser some infallible notes about the personal appearance of the great master, by which I might recognise him.

I took fresh courage, and determined not to delay my good fortune a day. It was impossible for me to meet Beethoven at his door, so I had found,—for in going out he always left his house by a rear door. So there was nothing left to me but the beer-garden. But, unfortunately, I sought the master there in vain, not only on this day, but on the next two following days also. Then, on the fourth, as I was once more directing my steps, at the proper hour, to the fateful beer-garden, I became to my utter consternation aware that the Englishman was dogging my steps, cautiously and suspiciously, at some distance behind me. The wretch, always on the lookout from his window, had not allowed it to escape him that I had been going out daily, always at the same hour, and always in the same direction. This, of course, struck him; and at once suspecting that I had run upon some secret path to find Beethoven, he had instantly determined to derive advantage from my supposed discovery.

He told me all this with the greatest candor, and declared, in the same breath, that he intended to follow me wherever I went. In vain I tried to deceive him and to have him believe that it was merely my intention to go to a beer-garden for some modest refreshment, much too unfashionable a place for a gentleman of his rank to care for. But he remained firm in his determination, and there was nothing left me but to curse my luck. Finally I tried the effect of incivility, attempting to drive him off with a gruff rudeness of speech. But far from suffering himself to be disconcerted or angered by it, he contented himself with a soft smile. It was his fixed idea to see Beethoven; he was indifferent to everything else.

And really this day it was to happen that I should see the great Beethoven for the first time. Nothing can describe my complete absorption, but at the same time my

utter wrath, as, sitting at the side of the English gentleman, I saw the man approach whose carriage and appearance so thoroughly corresponded with the descrip-
tion which the innkeeper had given me of the master:
the long, blue, great coat, the confusion of tangled gray
hair, and furthermore the glance and the expression of
countenance as they had long been accustomed to float
in my imagination, after a good portrait I had often seen.
A mistake was impossible. I recognised him on the instant. With short, rapid steps he approached and passed
before us. Awe and the suddenness of the surprise en-
chained my senses.

The Englishman lost none of my motions. He observed the new arrival curiously, who, retiring into the
farthest corner of the garden (at this hour but little frequented), ordered some wine, and then sat for some time
in a posture of thought. My loudly beating heart told
me: "It is he." I forgot my neighbor for some moments,
and gazed, with a greedy eye, and in an indescribable
state of emotion, at the man whose genius had ruled, to
the exclusion of everything else, over all my thoughts
and feelings ever since I had learned to think and feel.

Involuntarily I began to commune with myself in a low tone of voice and fell into a sort of monologue which closed with the words, only too portentous :

"Beethoven, it is you, then, whom I see before me?"

Nothing escaped my unhallowed neighbor, who, inclined closely to me, his breath repressed, had overheard my whispers. I was alarmed from my profound ecstasy by the words:—

"Yes! this gentleman is Beethoven! Come, let us introduce ourselves at once."

Filled both with anxiety and resentment, I clasped the accursed Englishman by the arm and restrained him.

"What is it you are about to do?" I cried. "Do you want to compromise both of us? Here in this place? So utterly forgetful of all propriety?"

"O," he rejoined, this is an excellent opportunity. We shall not easily find a better one."

Thereupon he drew from his pocket what appeared to be a manuscript roll of music, and was about to march directly upon the man in the blue great-coat. Entirely beside myself, I grasped the reckless man's coat-tails and shouted impetuously at him:—

"Are you crazy?"

This occurrence, brief as it was, had sufficed to attract the attention of the stranger. He seemed to guess, with a feeling of mortification, that he was the object of our excitement, and, hastily draining his glass, he arose to leave. Hardly had the Englishman observed the action, when he tore himself from my grasp with such force as to leave one of his coat-tails in my extended hand, and put himself in Beethoven's way. The latter sought to avoid by passing round him. But the good-for-nothing anticipated the purpose, bowed magnificently before him after the form prescribed by the latest English fashion, and addressed him as follows:—

"I have the honor to introduce myself to the very celebrated composer, the most honorable Herr Beethoven. "

He had no need to add more. For at the very first words, and after one sharp glance at myself, Beethoven, wheeling quickly to one side, disappeared with the quickness of a flash from the garden. Nothing daunted, however, the stolid Briton was for hastening after him, when I, in my furious wrath, could not refrain from laying violent hands on the remaining one of his coat-tails. He halted. The episode had in a measure astonished him, and he cried out in a queer tone of voice:—

"By Jove! This gentleman is worthy to be an Englishman! He is indeed a great man, and I shall not fail to make his acquaintance!"

I stood as one petrified. For me this dreadful adventure meant the destruction of all hope of ever seeing my heart's dearest wish fulfilled.

It was perfectly clear that henceforth every effort to approach Beethoven in the conventional way would be fruitless. In view of the state of my finances, now wholly ruinous, I was at length forced to make up my mind whether I should instantly start on my return homeward, leaving my designs unaccomplished, or whether in the hope of yet accomplishing them I should not attempt one final, desperate step more. I shuddered to the very bottom of my soul as I contemplated the former alternative. For who could, having after so much labor approached so closely to the very portals of the holy of holies, see them eternally closing against him, without being utterly prostrated?

I resolved, therefore, before I should wholly abandon my soul's salvation, to try yet some desperate step. But what was that step? What course should I pursue? For a long time I could think of nothing that promised success. Alas, my whole intellect had been lamed! Nothing offered itself to my excited phantasy, but the remembrance of what I had been compelled to endure, as I stood there, grasping with both my hands the rended coat-tail of the unspeakable Englishman. The sharp glance, which Beethoven had thrown askance toward my unhappy self at the very moment of this dread catastrophe, had not escaped me. I felt only too keenly, what was the meaning of that glance,—it had forever stamped me as an Englishman!

What should be my course to undeceive this suspicion of the master. Everything depended upon my succeeding in having him learn that I was but a simple German soul, full of terrestrial poverty, but celestial enthusiasm.

I decided, finally, to pour my whole heart out,—to write. This happened. I wrote; briefly related my life, how it was I had become a musician, how I worshipped him, how it was my humble suit to make his acquaintance, how I had sacrificed two whole years acquiring a name as a galop-composer, how I had entered upon and completed my pilgrimage, what misfortunes the Englishman had brought upon me, and how pitiful my present condition was.

And perceptibly feeling my heart grow lighter as I thus proceeded with the recital of my woes, the keen enjoyment of this feeling insensibly led me to adopt a style of respectful familiarity. I wove into the letter some very candid and rather forcible expressions of reproof against the unjust severity with which the master had seen fit to treat my poor self. I was virtually in an inspired state as at length I finished the letter. My eyes fairly swam as I wrote the address: "To Herr Ludwig von Beethoven." Then I breathed a heartfelt silent prayer, and myself delivered the letter at Beethoven's house.

As I was returning to the hotel, wrapt in my enthusiasm,—heavens! who was it, at this juncture, too, thrust that fearful Englishman upon my vision! From his window he had seen this latest of my journeys, also.

He read at once the joy with which hope had made my face radiant: that was enough to subject me to his spell again. Surely enough, he stopped me in the stairway with the inquiry:

"What hopes? Good? When shall we see Beethoven?"

"Never! Never!" I cried in desperation. "You,— Beethoven wishes never to see you again. Leave me, miserable sir! We have nothing in common."

"Yes, indeed, we have something in common," he replied, unmoved. "Where is my coat-tail, sir? Who authorised you to deprive me of it violently, as you did? Are you not aware that you are to blame that

Beethoven conducted himself toward me as he did? How could he, with any propriety, permit himself to form the acquaintance of a gentleman with but one coat-tail?"

I was exasperated at having this blame loaded upon my shoulders.

"Sir!" I shouted, "You shall have back your coat-tail! I trust you will preserve it, with feelings of shame, as a memento of how you mortally offended the great

Beethoven and plunged a poor musician into ruin. Farewell! and may we never see each other again!"

He sought to detain and calm me, assuring me that he still possessed a great number of coats in the very best condition. Only, I should let him know when Beethoven would receive us. Past all restraint, however, I stormed violently aloft to my fifth story. There I locked myself in and awaited Beethoven's answer.

How shall I describe what transpired within me, about me, when, really, within an hour or so, I received a small bit of note-paper upon which was written in a hasty hand:

"Pardon me, Mr. R., if I request that you will defer your call until to-morrow morning. I am busily engaged to-day in getting a packet of musical work ready for the next post. I shall look for you to-morrow. Beethoven."

First, I sank upon my knees and thanked Heaven for this extraordinary mark of favor; my eyes were dim with the most devoutly grateful tears. Then, at length, my feelings burst forth in the wildest demonstrations of joy, and I danced about in my little room like one bereft of reason. I do not recall what I was dancing, only that—

to my utter shame—I became suddenly conscious of whistling one of my own galops as an accompaniment. This mortifying discovery brought me to my senses. I forsook my little chamber and the hotel. Intoxicated with joy, I ran out into the streets of Vienna.

Wondrous Providence! My woes had caused me entirely to lose sight of the fact that I was in Vienna. But now, how the cheery bustle and activity of the inhabitants of the imperial city delighted me! Being in a state of enthusiasm, I saw everything through the enthusiast's eye. The rather shallow sensualism of the Viennese appeared to me to be the impulsive outbursts of ardent natures. Their light-hearted, not too discriminating lust of pleasure, I thought a spontaneous and candid responsiveness to all that is beautiful. I scanned the five daily announcements of the theatres. Lo! on one of them I read: "Fidelio, An Opera by Beethoven."

I at once made up my mind to go to this theatre, no matter to what appalling extent the profits of my galops had melted away. When I got to the cheap standing-room for which I could pay, the overture was just beginning. The opera was a revision of the earlier one,

which, under the title of "Leonore" had met with fail-
ure, much, I must say, to the credit of the profound
and discriminating Viennese public. I had never seen
a performance of the work in the form of "Leonore" ;
my great delight may therefore be imagined as I now
beheld the magnificent new opera at its initial appearance. It was a very young girl that rendered the Leonore; but despite her extreme youth, the songstress
seemed already to have become firmly wedded to the
genius of Beethoven. With what glowing ardor, what
poetry of feeling, what impressive effect she portrayed
this extraordinary woman! Her name was Wilhelmine
Schroeder. She it is who earned the high renown of
having revealed the depths of Beethoven's work to the
German public. Indeed, on this evening I saw her performance carry away even the superficial Viennese in a
rapture of enthusiasm. As for me, heaven itself seemed
to open. I was in a glory and worshipped that genius,
which—like Floristan—had led me forth from night to
light, from fetters to freedom.

I could not sleep that night. The recollection of what
I had just experienced, and the contemplation of what

awaited me on the morrow,—it was all too great and overwhelming to translate peacefully into the domain of dreams. I remained awake, revelling in anticipations and schooling myself for my appearance before Beethoven.

The momentous day on which I expected to meet Beethoven at last dawned. I waited impatiently for the proper hour for a morning call. It tolled at length and I went forth. The event of my life was about to happen. The thought of it made me quiver to my inmost being.

But I had a fearful ordeal yet to endure.

Sauntering at the door of Beethoven's house, my evil spirit coolly awaited me,—the Englishman! The wretch had been sowing his bribes right and left, and had at last corrupted even the host of our hotel. The latter had read Beethoven's unsealed lines to me, ere I had read them myself, and he had betrayed the contents to the Briton.

At the very sight of him, a cold perspiration started from all my pores. My poetic feeling vanished; the divine flame was quenched on the instant. Once more I was in his power.

"Come on!" thus the miserable man saluted me. "Let us introduce ourselves to Beethoven!"

I was first for throwing him off by recourse to a lie, pretending that I was not on my way to Beethoven at all. But he quickly cut off every such avenue of escape. With the utmost candor he acquainted me with the manner in which he had gotten possession of my secret, and affirmed that he would not again leave me until we both came away from Beethoven together. Then I endeavored to have him relinquish his intentions; first by kindly remonstrance,—in vain! Then I worked myself into a passion,—in vain! Finally, thinking to avoid him by fleetness of foot, I sped by him like an arrow, up the long stairway, and pulled like a madman at the doorbell. Ere the door was opened, the gentleman was again upon me, grasped the tails of my coat and cried:

"Don't attempt to run away from me. I have a claim upon your coat-tails and I shall maintain my hold on them till we are face to face with Beethoven."

I turned indignantly about, attempting to release myself from his grasp. Indeed, I even felt tempted to protect my person against the proud son of Britannia with acts of bodily violence. But the door just then opened. An old housekeeper appeared; her visage grew dark as she perceived us in our strange attitude, and she made a hasty motion as if to close the door upon us. In my great anxiety I shouted my name loudly, and protested that I had come upon the invitation of Herr Beethoven.

The old dame was still wavering, for the Englishman's appearance seemed to her to justify quite a deal of doubt, when suddenly Beethoven himself appeared at the door of his cabinet. Taking advantage of the moment, I stepped quickly within, advancing toward the master with the intention of excusing myself. But in doing so, I pulled the Englishman along with me, for he still obstinately clung to me. He carried out his purpose and released his hold of me only when we stood face to face with Beethoven. I made a low bow and stammered forth my name. Although he very probably did not hear it, still he seemed to know that I was the one who had written to him. He bade me enter his apartments. And without paying the least attention to Beethoven's look of amazement, my companion slipped stealthily in after me.

Here I was,—within the inmost holy place. But the horrible embarrassment into which the incorrigible Briton had thrown me, robbed me of all the calmness and self-collection which I had need of to enjoy my good fortune in a worthy manner. And Beethoven's exterior, too, was by no means of a kind to impress one agreeably or to put one altogether at ease. His dress—for wear within doors—was quite untidy. He wore a red flannel cloth girt about his body. His long, coarse gray hair fell unkempt about his head. And his grim inamicable countenance was by no means calculated to put an end to the embarrassment I felt. We took seats at a table covered with papers and quills.

Some moments of uncomfortable silence ensued. Neither of us spoke. Beethoven was plainly displeased at having received two persons instead of one.

At length, he broke the silence, asking me, in a voice that was grating and harsh :

"Are you from L . . . .?"

I was about to answer him, but he interrupted me, pushing a sheet of paper and a pencil toward me, and adding:

"Write! I do not hear!"

I knew of Beethoven's deafness and had prepared myself for it. Still it was like a stab through the heart to hear it in that harsh and broken voice of his, "I do not hear." To be solitary in the world, to live without joys and be poor, to know of no other escape from such a sordid life than that of the wondrous power of tones, and yet to have to say, "I do not hear!" Instantly I understood completely the external appearance of Beethoven, the wretchedness so deeply graven in his cheeks, the gloomy vindictiveness in his glance, the taciturn defiance on his lips: he did not hear!

Confused and hardly knowing what I wrote, I wrote down an entreaty for his pardon, together with a short explanation of the circumstances which had led to my coming in the company of the Englishman. The latter, in the meantime, had been sitting mute and contented, opposite Beethoven, who, after reading my lines, turned with considerable asperity upon him, demanding what he wished.

"I have the honor—" the Briton was beginning.

"I don't understand you," exclaimed Beethoven quickly interrupting him. "I do not hear, and I speak with some difficulty, too. Write down what you wish of me."

The Englishman reflected a moment, finally drew a delicate, pretty little piece of musical manuscript from his pocket, and said to me:

"It is well. Write, I beg Herr Beethoven to scan over my composition. Wherever he finds a place in it which does not please him, he will have the kindness to mark it with a cross."

I wrote down his request, word for word, in the hope that thus I might get rid of him. And so it happened. Beethoven, when he had read the request, laid the Englishman's composition upon the table, smiling grimly the while; then nodded and said:

"I shall send it."

My foreign gentleman was very well content with that. He arose, performed a most particularly splendid and formal bow and took his leave. I drew a deep breath of relief,—he was gone!

Now, indeed, I felt that I was within the sanctuary.

Even Beethoven's lineaments visibly brightened. He gazed calmly at me for a moment, and began:

"I suppose the Briton has caused you a great deal of annoyance? Let us offer solace to each other. Long ago, these touring Englishmen succeeded in tormenting me to the quick. They come to-day to see a poor musician, just as to-morrow they will flock to stare at some rare animal. I am very sorry, indeed, to have mistaken you for one of them. You wrote that you take pleasure in my compositions. It is a pleasure to me to hear it. For I no longer care much whether my works please the crowd or not."

This familiarity of address soon dispelled the embarrassment which oppressed me. I felt a thrill of joy at hearing these simple words. I wrote that surely I was not the only one who was filled with ardent enthusiasm for every one of his creations. That, for instance, I desired nothing more keenly than that I might secure for my native city the good fortune of some day seeing him visit it; and that he would then be very quickly convinced what a powerful impression upon the whole public his works had made there.

"I am quite willing to believe," replied Beethoven, "that my compositions find a more ready welcome in Northern Germany than they do here. I often lose patience with the people of Vienna. They listen daily to too much poor stuff to be in the humor—for any considerable length of time—to take up serious work in a serious manner."

I felt like contradicting this assertion and told him that I had been at the performance of "Fidelio," the evening before, and how the Vienna public had received the opera with the most evident enthusiasm.

"Hm! Hm!" muttered the master. "The 'Fidelio!' And yet I know that these folk are now clapping their hands out of sheer vanity. They are possessed of the notion that, in revising this opera, I have followed their counsel only. They wish to reward me for the trouble I have been to, and so cry, 'Bravo!' They are a good-natured people, though not overschooled. That is why I prefer to live among them rather than among people who are scholarly. Does the 'Fidelio' please you in its present form?"

I gave him an account of the impressions which the

performance had made upon me, and remarked that I thought the changes and additions had magnificently improved the work.

"A most disagreeable kind of labor!" rejoined Beethoven. "I am no composer of operas. At least, I know of no theatre in the world for which I should willingly write another opera. If I were to compose an opera after my own taste and views, people would run away from it. There would be no arias, duets, trios, nor any similar stuff in it, with which they patch operas together now-a-days. And that which I should put in their stead no singer would consent to sing, no public be willing to hear. They all know nothing better than the glittering falsehood, brilliant nonsense, sweet-coated ennui. He who were to attempt a true musical drama would be looked upon as a fool. He would, in fact, be a fool, if, after composing such a drama, he did not jealously keep it a secret, but sought to bring it before the people."

"And how would he have to proceed?" I asked, "to create such a musical drama."

"As Shakespeare did when he wrote his pieces," was the almost impetuous answer. Then, more self-contained, he continued: "When one is compelled to make it the main object to bedeck women, who have passable voices, with all kinds of gaudy tinsel, with which to obtain the bravos and the applause of clapping hands, he ought to turn a Parisian modiste, rather than go on as a dramatic composer. I, for my part, am not cut out for such buffoonery. I know that, on this account, the smart people think that, while I may know something about instrumental music, I shall never be at home in the composition of vocal music. And they are right, since they mean by vocal music operatic music only. And may heaven preserve me from ever feeling at home in composing such nonsense."

I took the liberty, here, of asking him if he really believed that any one who had once heard his "Adelaide" would venture to deny to him a most splendid capacity for vocal music, too.

"Well," he replied after a short pause, "the 'Adelaide' and similar pieces may, perhaps, be looked upon as trifles which are always opportune to the professional virtuosi, offering them the means they long for to display their excellent training and art. But why should not vocal music form a great and serious class of music apart, as well as instrumental music? Such, that we might demand as much respect for it from the careless singing folk as, for instance, is exacted of an orchestra in rendering a symphony. The human voice is an irrepressible fact. Moreover, it is a far more beautiful and noble medium of tone than any instrument of the orchestra. Then why may we not employ it with the same independence with which we do the orchestra? Think what new effects we might secure by such a procedure. For the special character of the human voice, because it is so wholly different from the peculiar qualities of the instruments, could very readily be rendered prominent and easily followed, and would thus permit of producing the most manifold combinations. The instruments are, as it were, the representatives of the primal media of the tones of creation and nature. That which they express can never be clearly defined or fixed; for they reproduce the very primal emotions themselves, just as they were born in the chaos of the first creation, when, perhaps, no such thing as a human being existed who could receive and give them an abiding place within his heart. The genius of the human voice is of an entirely different character. The human voice is the representative of the human heart and its sequestered, individual feeling. Its character is consequently limited, but at the same time definite and clear. Bring these two elemental classes together, now, and combine them! To the unrestrained primal emotions of nature, soaring away into the infinite (representing them by the instruments,) oppose the clear and determinate emotion of the human heart (representing it by the human voice). The presence of this latter element would have a benign and pacificatory effect upon the war of what I have styled nature's primal emotions; would give to their various and uncertain streams a fixed and united course. And, on its own side, in becoming receptive of these primal emotions of nature, the human heart, immeasurably strengthened and expanded, would become capable of perceiving clearly within itself the supreme,—theretofore felt but as an uncertain instinct, but now transformed into a divine consciousness."

Here Beethoven discontinued for a few moments, as though exhausted. Then he proceeded, sighing gently:—

"Of course, in attempting to solve this problem, we encounter many difficulties. To render expression in song, words are necessary. But who would be capable of expressing, in words, a poetry which is founded on such a union of all elements? The poet's art must retire before such a task: words are too weakly media for its performance.—You will, sir, soon see a new composition of mine, which will remind you of what I have just been saying. It is a symphony with choruses. I call your attention to the difficulty I met while composing it, in the effort to surmount the obstacle caused by the inadequacy of poetry when I sought its aid. I finally decided to use Schiller's beautiful hymn, An die Freude. This is, indeed, a noble and exalted poem, although it falls far short of expressing that to which, in this case, it is true, no verses in the world can give adequate expression."

To this very day I can hardly comprehend all the joy I felt as Beethoven thus himself assisted me, with these brief hints, to the thorough understanding of his titanic last symphony which was then, at most, but just finished, but as yet known to no one. I expressed my

warmest gratitude for this surely most unusual conde-
scension; giving utterance at the same time to the delight which his information afforded me that another
great work of his might soon be expected. The tears had
started to my eyes. I could have knelt before him.

Beethoven seemed to note my deep emotion. He
looked at me, smiling half sadly, half mockingly, as he
said:

"You can defend me when the discussion of my new
work arises. Remember what I say: the wise folk will
deem me mad, or at least hoot at me as such. But you
see, Mr. R—, that I am not exactly a mad-man yet, although in other respects I am unfortunate enough to be
one.—People demand that I shall write as they imagine it is beautiful and good; they do not consider that I,
poor deaf wretch, must necessarily have peculiar ideas
of my own,—that it is impossible for me to compose
otherwise than as I feel. And that I cannot think their
beautiful thoughts nor feel their nice feelings," he add-
ed ironically, "that is just my misfortune!"

With that he arose, and with short, rapid steps strode
up and down the room. Deeply moved to my inmost

being as I was, I, too, arose; I felt that I was trembling. Impossible it would have been for me to have continued the conversation, either in pantomime or in writing. I became conscious that now the moment had come when my visit, if protracted, might weary the master. To write it down seemed to me too vapid a manner of expressing my thanks and saying farewell. I contented myself with reaching for my hat, stepping before Beethoven, and letting him read in my glance what was passing within me.

He seemed to understand me.

"You are going?" he asked. "Shall you remain any length of time in Vienna?"

I wrote for him to read that I had no other purpose in making this journey than to become acquainted with him; that since he had honored me by according me such an unusual reception, I was beyond measure happy to view my object as accomplished, and should on the morrow begin my journey homeward.

He rejoined, with a smile: "In your letter you told me in what way you created the funds for this journey. You ought to remain at Vienna and continue your composition of galops. This class of music is highly esteemed here."

I declared that I was done with it for good; that I knew of nothing which could ever again appear worth the sacrifice.

"Well, well!" he rejoined, "time will tell. I, too, old simpleton that I am, would be better off if I composed galops. If I go on as I have been I shall always more or less be in want. A happy journey!" he continued. "Remember me, and in all the hardships you may encounter, console yourself with me."

Agitated and with tears in my eyes, I was about to take my leave, when he suddenly called to me: " Hold! let us finish off the musical Englishman first! Let us see where the crosses shall come!"

He seized the Briton's manuscript, scanned it hastily over, smiling the while. Then he carefully gathered it together again, rolled it up in a sheet of paper, grasped a coarse pen, and drew a colossal cross over the whole wrapping. Then he handed it to me, with the words:—

"There! kindly hand the lucky fellow his masterpiece! He is an ass, and yet I envy him his long ears!—

Farewell, dear sir, and keep me in kind remembrance!"

Then he let me go. I was overcome as I left the room and the house.

In the hotel, I came across the Englishman's serving man packing away his master's trunks in the travelling coach. Evidently his object had been attained, too; I was forced to admit that he also had shown pertinacity. I hurried to my room and likewise got ready to begin my return journey afoot, with the dawn of the coming day. I laughed aloud as I gazed at the cross upon the wrapping round the Englishman's composition. And yet this cross was a souvenir of Beethoven, and I was loth that the evil spirit of my pilgrimage should possess it. I came to a quick decision, I took the wrapping off, brought out my galops and hid them away in this damning cover. I had the Englishman's composition taken to him without any cover, and accompanied it with a note in which I informed him that Beethoven had envied him and had affirmed he knew not a single spot at which to make a cross.

As I was leaving the hotel, I saw my quondam companion getting into his wagon.

"Farewell!" he called to me. "You have done me a great service. I am very glad to have made the acquaintance of Mr. Beethoven.—Would you like to go with me to Italy?"

"What are you looking for there?" I asked in reply.

"I want to make the acquaintance of Mr. Rossini. For he is a very celebrated composer."

"Good luck!" I cried. "I know Beethoven. That is enough for me so long as I live!"

We separated. I threw yet one yearning glance at Beethoven's house and journeyed toward the North, in my heart exalted and ennobled.

The Codes Of Hammurabi And Moses
W. W. Davies

QTY

The discovery of the Hammurabi Code is one of the greatest achievements of archaeology, and is of paramount interest, not only to the student of the Bible, but also to all those interested in ancient history...

Religion   ISBN: *1-59462-338-4*   **Pages:132**
MSRP $12.95

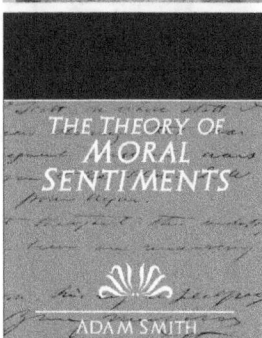

The Theory of Moral Sentiments
Adam Smith

QTY

This work from 1749. contains original theories of conscience amd moral judgment and it is the foundation for systemof morals.

Philosophy ISBN: *1-59462-777-0*   **Pages:536**
MSRP $19.95

Jessica's First Prayer
Hesba Stretton

QTY

In a screened and secluded corner of one of the many railway-bridges which span the streets of London there could be seen a few years ago, from five o'clock every morning until half past eight, a tidily set-out coffee-stall, consisting of a trestle and board, upon which stood two large tin cans, with a small fire of charcoal burning under each so as to keep the coffee boiling during the early hours of the morning when the work-people were thronging into the city on their way to their daily toil...

Pages:84

Childrens   ISBN: *1-59462-373-2*   *MSRP $9.95*

My Life and Work
Henry Ford

QTY

Henry Ford revolutionized the world with his implementation of mass production for the Model T automobile. Gain valuable business insight into his life and work with his own auto-biography... "We have only started on our development of our country we have not as yet, with all our talk of wonderful progress, done more than scratch the surface. The progress has been wonderful enough but..."

Pages:300

Biographies/   ISBN: *1-59462-198-5*   *MSRP $21.95*

The Art of Cross-Examination
Francis Wellman

QTY

I presume it is the experience of every author, after his first book is published upon an important subject, to be almost overwhelmed with a wealth of ideas and illustrations which could readily have been included in his book, and which to his own mind, at least, seem to make a second edition inevitable. Such certainly was the case with me; and when the first edition had reached its sixth impression in five months, I rejoiced to learn that it seemed to my publishers that the book had met with a sufficiently favorable reception to justify a second and considerably enlarged edition. ..

Reference **ISBN: *1-59462-647-2***

Pages:412

MSRP $19.95

On the Duty of Civil Disobedience
Henry David Thoreau

QTY

Thoreau wrote his famous essay, On the Duty of Civil Disobedience, as a protest against an unjust but popular war and the immoral but popular institution of slave-owning. He did more than write—he declined to pay his taxes, and was hauled off to gaol in consequence. Who can say how much this refusal of his hastened the end of the war and of slavery ?

Law **ISBN: *1-59462-747-9***

Pages:48

MSRP $7.45

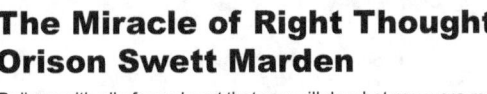

Dream Psychology Psychoanalysis for Beginners
Sigmund Freud

QTY

Sigmund Freud, born Sigismund Schlomo Freud (May 6, 1856 - September 23, 1939), was a Jewish-Austrian neurologist and psychiatrist who co-founded the psychoanalytic school of psychology. Freud is best known for his theories of the unconscious mind, especially involving the mechanism of repression; his redefinition of sexual desire as mobile and directed towards a wide variety of objects; and his therapeutic techniques, especially his understanding of transference in the therapeutic relationship and the presumed value of dreams as sources of insight into unconscious desires.

Psychology **ISBN: *1-59462-905-6***

Pages:196

MSRP $15.45

The Miracle of Right Thought
Orison Swett Marden

QTY

Believe with all of your heart that you will do what you were made to do. When the mind has once formed the habit of holding cheerful, happy, prosperous pictures, it will not be easy to form the opposite habit. It does not matter how improbable or how far away this realization may see, or how dark the prospects may be, if we visualize them as best we can, as vividly as possible, hold tenaciously to them and vigorously struggle to attain them, they will gradually become actualized, realized in the life. But a desire, a longing without endeavor, a yearning abandoned or held indifferently will vanish without realization.

Pages:360

Self Help **ISBN: *1-59462-644-8***

MSRP $25.45

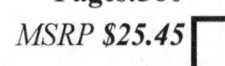

The Rosicrucian Cosmo-Conception Mystic Christianity by *Max Heindel*   ISBN: *1-59462-188-8*   **$38.95**
The Rosicrucian Cosmo-conception is not dogmatic, neither does it appeal to any other authority than the reason of the student. It is: not controversial, but is: sent forth in the, hope that it may help to clear...   New Age/Religion Pages 646

Abandonment To Divine Providence by *Jean-Pierre de Caussade*   ISBN: *1-59462-228-0*   **$25.95**
"The Rev. Jean Pierre de Caussade was one of the most remarkable spiritual writers of the Society of Jesus in France in the 18th Century. His death took place at Toulouse in 1751. His works have gone through many editions and have been republished...   Inspirational/Religion Pages 400

Mental Chemistry by *Charles Haanel*   ISBN: *1-59462-192-6*   **$23.95**
Mental Chemistry allows the change of material conditions by combining and appropriately utilizing the power of the mind. Much like applied chemistry creates something new and unique out of careful combinations of chemicals the mastery of mental chemistry...   New Age Pages 354

The Letters of Robert Browning and Elizabeth Barret Barrett 1845-1846 vol II   ISBN: *1-59462-193-4*   **$35.95**
by *Robert Browning* and *Elizabeth Barrett*   Biographies Pages 596

Gleanings In Genesis (volume I) by *Arthur W. Pink*   ISBN: *1-59462-130-6*   **$27.45**
Appropriately has Genesis been termed "the seed plot of the Bible" for in it we have, in germ form, almost all of the great doctrines which are afterwards fully developed in the books of Scripture which follow...   Religion/Inspirational Pages 420

The Master Key by *L. W. de Laurence*   ISBN: *1-59462-001-6*   **$30.95**
In no branch of human knowledge has there been a more lively increase of the spirit of research during the past few years than in the study of Psychology, Concentration and Mental Discipline. The requests for authentic lessons in Thought Control, Mental Discipline and...   New Age/Business Pages 422

The Lesser Key Of Solomon Goetia by *L. W. de Laurence*   ISBN: *1-59462-092-X*   **$9.95**
This translation of the first book of the "Lernegton" which is now for the first time made accessible to students of Talismanic Magic was done, after careful collation and edition, from numerous Ancient Manuscripts in Hebrew, Latin, and French...   New Age/Occult Pages 92

Rubaiyat Of Omar Khayyam by *Edward Fitzgerald*   ISBN:*1-59462-332-5*   **$13.95**
Edward Fitzgerald, whom the world has already learned, in spite of his own efforts to remain within the shadow of anonymity, to look upon as one of the rarest poets of the century, was born at Bredfield, in Suffolk, on the 31st of March, 1809. He was the third son of John Purcell...   Music Pages 172

Ancient Law by *Henry Maine*   ISBN: *1-59462-128-4*   **$29.95**
The chief object of the following pages is to indicate some of the earliest ideas of mankind, as they are reflected in Ancient Law, and to point out the relation of those ideas to modern thought.   Religion/History Pages 452

Far-Away Stories by *William J. Locke*   ISBN: *1-59462-129-2*   **$19.45**
"Good wine needs no bush, but a collection of mixed vintages does. And this book is just such a collection. Some of the stories I do not want to remain buried for ever in the museum files of dead magazine-numbers an author's not unpardonable vanity..."   Fiction Pages 272

Life of David Crockett by *David Crockett*   ISBN: *1-59462-250-7*   **$27.45**
"Colonel David Crockett was one of the most remarkable men of the times in which he lived. Born in humble life, but gifted with a strong will, an indomitable courage, and unremitting perseverance...   Biographies/New Age Pages 424

Lip-Reading by *Edward Nitchie*   ISBN: *1-59462-206-X*   **$25.95**
Edward B. Nitchie, founder of the New York School for the Hard of Hearing, now the Nitchie School of Lip-Reading, Inc, wrote "LIP-READING Principles and Practice". The development and perfecting of this meritorious work on lip-reading was an undertaking...   How-to Pages 400

A Handbook of Suggestive Therapeutics, Applied Hypnotism, Psychic Science   ISBN: *1-59462-214-0*   **$24.95**
by *Henry Munro*   Health/New Age/Health/Self-help Pages 376

A Doll's House: and Two Other Plays by *Henrik Ibsen*   ISBN: *1-59462-112-8*   **$19.95**
Henrik Ibsen created this classic when in revolutionary 1848 Rome. Introducing some striking concepts in playwriting for the realist genre, this play has been studied the world over.   Fiction/Classics/Plays 308

The Light of Asia by *sir Edwin Arnold*   ISBN: *1-59462-204-3*   **$13.95**
In this poetic masterpiece, Edwin Arnold describes the life and teachings of Buddha. The man who was to become known as Buddha to the world was born as Prince Gautama of India but he rejected the worldly riches and abandoned the reigns of power when...   Religion/History/Biographies Pages 170

The Complete Works of Guy de Maupassant by *Guy de Maupassant*   ISBN: *1-59462-157-8*   **$16.95**
"For days and days, nights and nights, I had dreamed of that first kiss which was to consecrate our engagement, and I knew not on what spot I should put my lips..."   Fiction/Classics Pages 240

The Art of Cross-Examination by *Francis L. Wellman*   ISBN: *1-59462-309-0*   **$26.95**
Written by a renowned trial lawyer, Wellman imparts his experience and uses case studies to explain how to use psychology to extract desired information through questioning.   How-to/Science/Reference Pages 408

Answered or Unanswered? by *Louisa Vaughan*   ISBN: *1-59462-248-5*   **$10.95**
Miracles of Faith in China   Religion Pages 112

The Edinburgh Lectures on Mental Science (1909) by *Thomas*   ISBN: *1-59462-008-3*   **$11.95**
This book contains the substance of a course of lectures recently given by the writer in the Queen Street Hail, Edinburgh. Its purpose is to indicate the Natural Principles governing the relation between Mental Action and Material Conditions...   New Age/Psychology Pages 148

Ayesha by *H. Rider Haggard*   ISBN: *1-59462-301-5*   **$24.95**
Verily and indeed it is the unexpected that happens! Probably if there was one person upon the earth from whom the Editor of this, and of a certain previous history, did not expect to hear again...   Classics Pages 380

Ayala's Angel by *Anthony Trollope*   ISBN: *1-59462-352-X*   **$29.95**
The two girls were both pretty, but Lucy who was twenty-one who supposed to be simple and comparatively unattractive, whereas Ayala was credited, as her Bombwhat romantic name might show, with poetic charm and a taste for romance. Ayala when her father died was nineteen...   Fiction Pages 484

The American Commonwealth by *James Bryce*   ISBN: *1-59462-286-8*   **$34.45**
An interpretation of American democratic political theory. It examines political mechanics and society from the perspective of Scotsman James Bryce   Politics Pages 572

Stories of the Pilgrims by *Margaret P. Pumphrey*   ISBN: *1-59462-116-0*   **$17.95**
This book explores pilgrims religious oppression in England as well as their escape to Holland and eventual crossing to America on the Mayflower, and their early days in New England...   History Pages 268

QTY

The Fasting Cure *by Sinclair Upton*　　　　　　　　　　　ISBN: *1-59462-222-1*　**$13.95**
In the Cosmopolitan Magazine for May, 1910, and in the Contemporary Review (London) for April, 1910, I published an article dealing with my experi-
ences in fasting. I have written a great many magazine articles, but never one which attracted so much attention...　New Age/Self Help/Health Pages 164

Hebrew Astrology *by Sepharial*　　　　　　　　　　　　　ISBN: *1-59462-308-2*　**$13.45**
In these days of advanced thinking it is a matter of common observation that we have left many of the old landmarks behind and that we are now pressing
forward to greater heights and to a wider horizon than that which represented the mind-content of our progenitors...　Astrology Pages 144

Thought Vibration or The Law of Attraction in the Thought World　　　ISBN: *1-59462-127-6*　**$12.95**

by William Walker Atkinson　　　　　　　　　　　　　　　　*Psychology/Religion Pages 144*

Optimism *by Helen Keller*　　　　　　　　　　　　　　　ISBN: *1-59462-108-X*　**$15.95**
Helen Keller was blind, deaf, and mute since 19 months old, yet famously learned how to overcome these handicaps, communicate with the world, and
spread her lectures promoting optimism. An inspiring read for everyone...　Biographies/Inspirational Pages 84

Sara Crewe *by Frances Burnett*　　　　　　　　　　　　ISBN: *1-59462-360-0*　**$9.45**
In the first place, Miss Minchin lived in London. Her home was a large, dull, tall one, in a large, dull square, where all the houses were alike, and all the
sparrows were alike, and where all the door-knockers made the same heavy sound...　Childrens/Classic Pages 88

The Autobiography of Benjamin Franklin *by Benjamin Franklin*　　ISBN: *1-59462-135-7*　**$24.95**
The Autobiography of Benjamin Franklin has probably been more extensively read than any other American historical work, and no other book of its kind
has had such ups and downs of fortune. Franklin lived for many years in England, where he was agent...　Biographies/History Pages 332

Name	
Email	
Telephone	
Address	
City, State ZIP	

☐ **Credit Card**　　　　☐ **Check / Money Order**

Credit Card Number	
Expiration Date	
Signature	

Please Mail to:　Book Jungle
PO Box 2226
Champaign, IL 61825
or Fax to:　　　630-214-0564

ORDERING INFORMATION

web: *www.bookjungle.com*
email: *sales@bookjungle.com*
fax: *630-214-0564*
mail: *Book Jungle PO Box 2226 Champaign, IL 61825*
or PayPal *to sales@bookjungle.com*

Please contact us for bulk discounts

DIRECT-ORDER TERMS

**20% Discount if You Order
Two or More Books**
Free Domestic Shipping!
Accepted: Master Card, Visa,
Discover, American Express

www.ingramcontent.com/pod-product-compliance
Lightning Source LLC
Chambersburg PA
CBHW081305200626
46813CB00018B/3263